MEGAN'S YEAR

An Irish Traveler's Story

Written by *Gloria Whelan* and Illustrated by *Beth Peck*

Tales of the World *from* Sleeping Bear Press

IRELAND

To Eva Nolan
—Gloria

For Emma and Anna Rose
—Beth

Sleeping Bear Press
315 E. Eisenhower Pkwy., Suite 200
Ann Arbor, MI 48108
www.sleepingbearpress.com

Sleeping Bear Press is an imprint of Gale, a part of Cengage Learning.

10 9 8 7 6 5 4 3 2 1

Printed by China Translation & Printing Services Limited,
Guangdong Province, China. 1st printing. 04/2011

Library of Congress Cataloging-in-Publication Data

Whelan, Gloria.
Megan's year : an Irish Traveler's story / written by Gloria Whelan ;
illustrated by Beth Peck.
p. cm.
Summary: Ten-year-old Megan Brady tells of her family's lifestyle, spending
summers traveling in a caravan through the Irish countryside getting work
where they can, and winters in Dublin so the children can attend school.
ISBN 978-1-58536-449-7
1. Irish Travellers (Nomadic people)–Juvenile fiction. 2. Ireland–Juvenile
fiction. [1. Irish Travellers (Nomadic people)–Fiction. 2. Family life–Ireland–
Fiction. 3. Ireland–Fiction.] I. Peck, Beth, ill. II. Title.
PZ7.W5718Meg 2011
[Fic]–dc22   2010052914

There are two of me, the winter Megan Brady and the summer Megan Brady. It's summer in Ireland now and we live in a house that travels with us. When winter comes we'll live in a *tigin*, a house that stays in one place.

When I complain that my life is too mixed up, Daddy points to the swallows, arrowing back and forth in the sky.

"Megan," he says, "the swallows are Travelers like we are. They are here all summer, and then like us they fly away when winter comes."

Do the swallows like it here or where they go in the winter? I think of a swallow shut up in a school, beating its wings against the window.

For longer than anyone can remember our folks have wandered the roads of Ireland. When Daddy was a boy he lived in a barrel wagon drawn by a horse. I'd like that better than our old caravan that breaks down all the time. The *garda* tells us to move along. The *buffers* laugh at us and call us tinkers. "Tinkers" is a name they give us because we Travelers used to go from village to village to repair tin kettles and buckets.

Like me, Daddy is happiest on the road. You know all about the place where you are, but what's ahead can be anything you want it to be, so there's never any bad in it.

Today we park in Mr. O'Connor's field. Daddy will give O'Connor a hand with cultivating the potato field like he did last year. My sisters and brothers and I tumble out of the dusty caravan and run for O'Connor's pond, our dog, Willie, at our heels.

We're hot from being shut up all day. We jump in the pond. Nine-year-old Maeve slips through the water like an otter. Mary is five and stays where it's shallow. I'm ten. I turn on my back and float. I look up at the sky and watch the clouds turn into sheep. Tim and Jimmy are twins. They're twelve and busy ducking each other and splashing us. Willie is in the pond and then out, shaking off the water.

When we get back to the caravan, wet and shivering, Daddy and Mammy are waiting for us. Mammy says, "Get yourselves dried off and into your clothes. We're moving on."

"O'Connor got himself a machine to cultivate his crops," Daddy says. "He's no need of me." Jimmy and Tim beg to stay on for another day but Daddy uses his angry voice to tell them to hurry up. "We're not staying where we're not wanted," he says, climbing into the caravan and slamming the door.

There's more and more places we can't go. One of them is the Gormans' farm where Daddy used to dig turf and stack it for the winter to feed their fireplace. Last year Mr. Gorman and his neighbors bought themselves a machine to do the work.

It's dark when Daddy finally pulls into a campground. Mammy's happy because it's got a water faucet and I'm happy because it's got an outhouse and I don't have to go in the field.

There's two other Travelers' caravans parked nearby. We hear a fiddle and pipes. It's a party for sure. We head for their campfire. Travelers are happiest when they are with other Travelers. We trust one another more than we trust *buffers*.

I smell something delicious. Pig roasting. There'll be food for us because Travelers are never strangers to one another. Mammy and Daddy are sure to find they are related to someone. That's the way with Travelers.

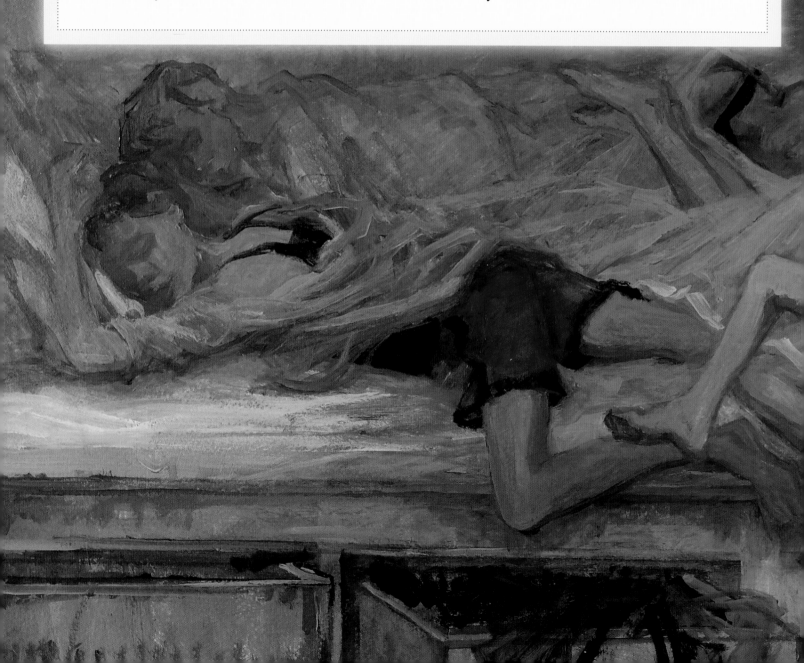

The fiddler and piper play. There's singing, some of the words in *Gammon*, which is our Travelers' secret language. We never tell anyone what a *Gammon* word means unless they are one of us. There are songs and stories of the old days. We Travelers don't have history books but we have our songs and stories.

My favorite stories are ghost stories. There's plenty of ghost stories this night and my sisters and I all sleep tight together.

Next day we get a bit of luck. Mr. Flynn needs Daddy's help putting on a new roof. That's good news because it means we can park in his field for a week. There's a stream with fish on the property. Flynn lets us kids keep half of what we catch. The other half goes to him.

We're out the door, breakfast in our hands. The stream runs cold and clear like a chip of ice. We step into the water with our fishing poles and moan and groan until we get used to the cold. I get the first fish. It's a trout, slippery with wanting to get away, its belly speckled in rainbow colors.

Flynn pays us for picking his raspberries. Mrs. Flynn keeps a sharp eye to be sure we don't eat them. Afterward we go off into the heath to find wild bilberries. We stick out our purple tongues and make each other laugh.

Now it's cleaning chimneys and mucking out stables and any dirty job that will bring a euro or two. We're on the road most of the time until the white flowers of the potato plants drop off and it's time to dig potatoes. Tim and Jimmy and me are out in the fields. Our knees are sore from kneeling and we'll never get the dirt out from under our nails. When everyone is paid, the twins and me get five euros each.

Leaves blow across the roads and the fields are dotted with flocking blackbirds. The cuckoo is long gone and so are the swallows. We're off to the big city of Dublin. It's time for the winter Megan.

Mammy says there's no learning for us in the country and we kids just run wild. She's happiest in the city where you can turn on and off the river of water that hides in the pipes. With a flick of a switch you can make the sun shine in the house. If we're hungry there's a building where you ride an elevator to an office and they give you money for food.

Daddy says it's unhealthy in the city with bad air that's all used up and how can he keep an eye on us kids in the city? Who knows what trouble we'll get into sitting around watching the telly in somebody's house? He doesn't like taking the handout from the building with the elevators. In the summer he can find work. In the city no one wants him. In the city there's no place to go and nothing to do that doesn't cost money.

We live scrunched together in our *tigin*, one of two dozen that are all alike. You have to look at the numbers to be sure you're home. Shut inside is like being in prison. Three of us girls sleep in one bed; my two brothers in another. Willie won't come inside but curls up under the caravan. He wants to be sure we won't leave without him.

Daddy goes from yard to yard collecting scrap metal to sell. Mammy goes from house to house asking for used clothes. One day she got me a velvet dress but most of the time Mammy sells what she gets to help toward our school uniforms and books.

We go to St. John's National School. Daddy stayed late cutting oats so I'm two weeks behind in my class. In the hall Bridget gives me a push and calls me a stupid tinker. She laughs at me because my uniform is last year's and too short.

I call Bridget a name in *Gammon*. Sister Joseph frowns but she doesn't know what I've said. She tells Bridget she lacks charity and has her stay after school and write out twenty times: *And now abideth faith, hope, charity, these three; but the greatest of these is charity.*

Sister Joseph tells Bridget, "Our Lord was often on the road."

Sister has me stay after school to help me catch up with my reading. I ask her, "Have you got a book with summer in it?"

Tim's learning to be an electrician. Yesterday he took a radio someone threw away and made it work. He likes Dublin and says it's where he'll live when he's grown.

Jimmy is on the hurling team at school. Hurling is played with sticks and a ball that can go 150 kilometers a minute. He wants to live in a city and get on a professional team.

Daddy doesn't like it that his boys won't be on the road. I tell him I will be, for sure.

This morning I'm in the computer room at school. I get restless and stare out the window. It's April and the summer birds are returning. Yesterday I saw my first swallow. The buds on the trees are showing green and the rain this morning on the way to school was warm. In Flynn's stream the fish will be jumping for the spring bugs. On the farms they'll be plowing the potato beds.

Sister taps me on the shoulder. "You're daydreaming again, Megan," she says. "What are you thinking of?"

I tell her I'm dreaming of summer and being on the road.

She shows me how I can get pictures on the computer of places all over the world. "That's a kind of traveling, too, Megan," she says.

Home from school I see Daddy working on the caravan. I climb inside the caravan. There's our cooking pot and skillet. I think of all the campfires we sat around, watching the sun turn gold and slip behind the hills. I remember falling asleep in the caravan at night and then awakening first thing in the morning to see where we are. Is it someplace we want to be? Or a place we've never been before? What will it be like?

I stick my head out the window and tell Daddy I can't wait until we take off. Daddy says even when we're living in the *tigin* we are still Travelers in our hearts. That's true, for though my two feet are in Dublin, my heart is already hurrying down a road toward summer.

AUTHOR'S NOTE

There are approximately 25 thousand Travelers (spelled *Travellers* in England and Ireland) in Ireland. Forced off their meager farms by English landlords and by the potato famines, the Irish took to the roads. Some found itinerant (moving from place to place) life to their liking. They married other Travelers and over the years a culture of traveling developed.

As farm acreage turns into suburbs, Travelers are giving up their way of life and migrating to the cities. The Irish government has tried to provide accommodation for Travelers and the schools make a special effort to meet the needs of their children.

Like Megan's father, my father liked the roads. On our vacations, even after a long day's drive, my father set off with us to explore our new surroundings. "Let's mosey around," he would say. My father instilled a wanderlust in me I share with Megan.

GLOSSARY

Buffers: outsiders (people with permanent homes)

Caravan: camper or trailer

Euro: the currency of Ireland and of the countries in the European Union

Gammon: a secret language used by Travelers, sometimes called *Shelta*

Garda: the Irish police

Tigin (also tigeen): the Irish word for a small hut or house

Turf: dried-out peat sod used for fuel in fireplaces